Freddie's Christmas Letter

by Audrey Tarrant

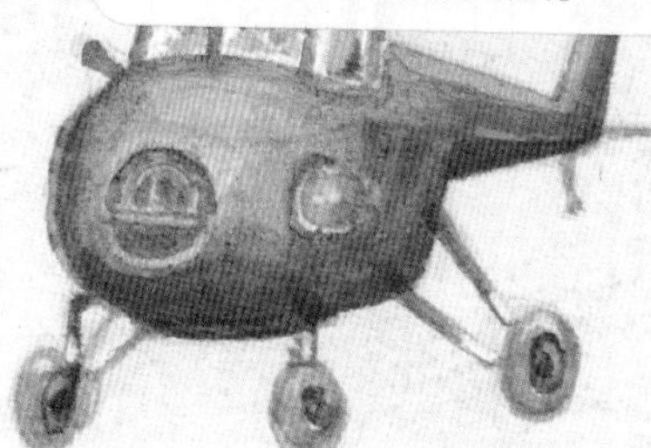

 Printed in England ISBN 0 85503 179 4

Freddie the teddy and Flora sat on the window-sill writing a letter to Father Christmas.

'He lives at the North Pole,' said Freddie. He put his letter in his pocket and leant out of the window.

Freddie was sure there was a post box
just by the side gate.
He leant out further,
his paws slipped on the snowy ledge
. . . . . and he fell.
Flora grabbed Freddie's trouser leg,
she slipped too and . . . . . whoosh . . . .
both bears slid down the roof
and landed safely in the soft snow
on the flower tub.

‘Now we are out we can post the letter,’ said Flora.
They ran down the path and through the gate.
But the post box was too high and,
even when Flora stood on Freddie’s shoulders,
she still could not reach it.

GR

Then Freddie had a bright idea.

'Let's go and find the North Pole and GIVE Father Christmas our letter,' he said.

'The Woodland Bus goes to North Pine Station, and that must be somewhere near the North Pole'. The bus driver did not know where the North Pole was, but he told them to ask at the station.

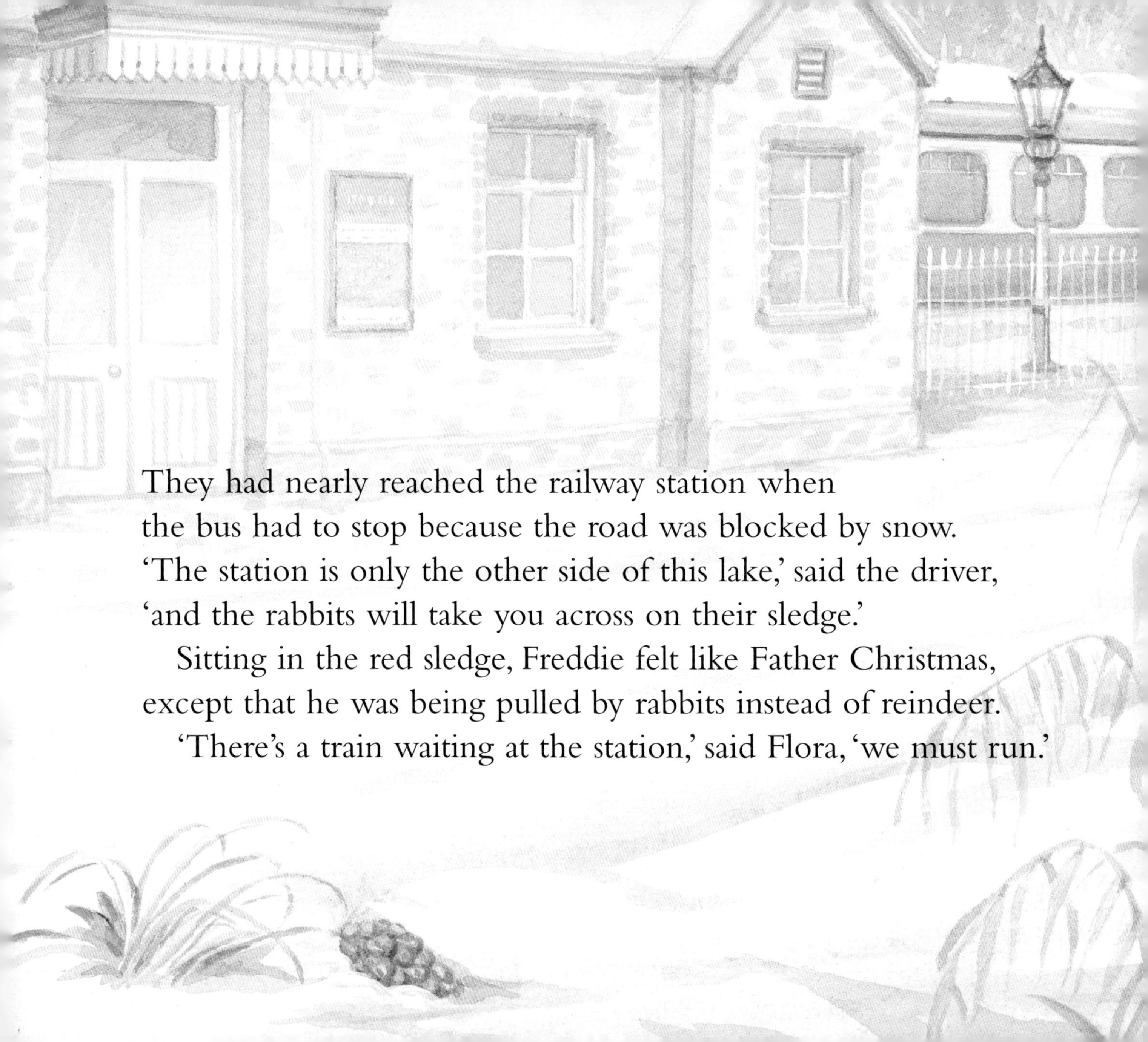

They had nearly reached the railway station when
the bus had to stop because the road was blocked by snow.
'The station is only the other side of this lake,' said the driver,
'and the rabbits will take you across on their sledge.'

Sitting in the red sledge, Freddie felt like Father Christmas,
except that he was being pulled by rabbits instead of reindeer.

'There's a train waiting at the station,' said Flora, 'we must run.'

‘This train goes to North Field,’
said the guard, ‘but if you ask the Station Master
when you get there, I’m sure he will know.
All aboard!’

But when they reached North Field
they did not have to ask the Station Master,
for there, on the top of the hill,
they could see a small house
with a pole beside it flying a flag!

‘That MUST be the North Pole,’
cried Freddie.

NOR

They puffed and panted their way up the steep hill. It WAS a long way. They knocked on the door, but no-one was at home.

'Perhaps Father Christmas has gone to fetch all the presents,' said Flora as Freddie posted his letter through the front door.

They trudged their way back down the hill. 'Oh dear,' said Flora, 'I do feel tired.'

'Yes, and my feet hurt,' said Freddie. There was a loud squeak as Flora suddenly fell into deep snow up to her chin. Freddie heaved and tugged, but he could not pull her out. Oh dear! What could they do?

They were getting tired and worried when they heard a loud whirring noise, and Mr Hare's Rescue Helicopter hovered over them. He spotted them, and soon both Flora and Freddie were winched up into the helicopter.

The helicopter flew them all the way home and landed in the field beside the house. Luckily the back door was open, and no-one saw them creep inside.

What a wonderful adventure just to post a letter!

On Christmas Eve Freddie and Flora
hung up their stockings.
After everyone was asleep,
they crept out of bed
and looked out of the window.
There, in the sky, was Father Christmas
coming towards the house.
They jumped back into bed,
and pulled the covers over their heads.

On Christmas morning when they woke up, their stockings were full of the very presents they had asked for.

What do you think they were?

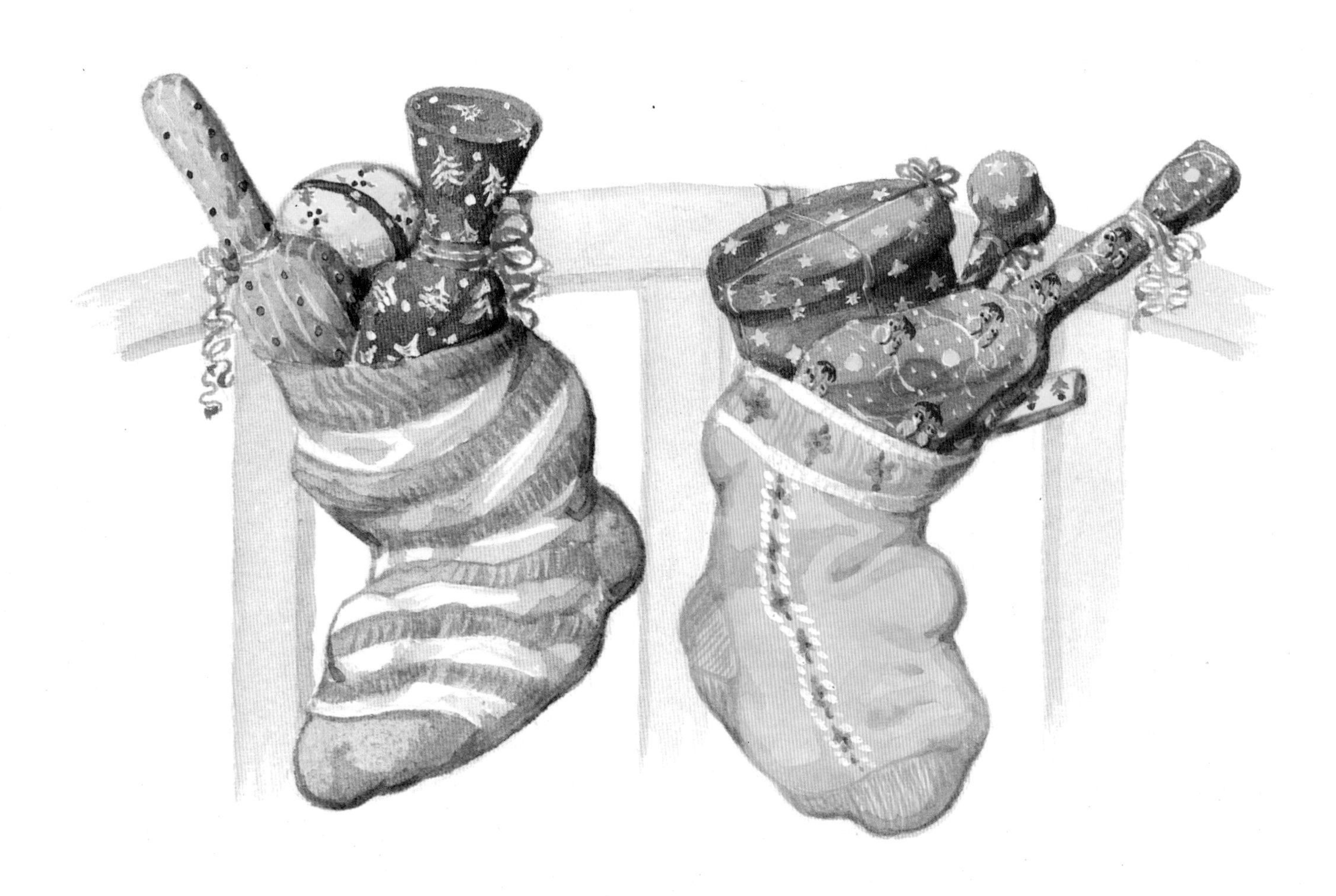